Train Is ready to depart · · ·

Board it NOW!

Local Passenger

Short Stories based on Indian Railway Journeys

By

Shardul Dave

ISBN 978-93-5416-831-4

Published in India 2020 by Pencil

A brand of
One Point Six Technologies Pvt. Ltd.
123, Building J2, Shram Seva Premises,
Wadala Truck Terminal, Wadala (E)
Mumbai 400037, Maharashtra, INDIA
E connect@thepencilapp.com
W www.thepencilapp.com

DISCLAIMER: *This is a work of fiction. Names, characters, places, events and incidents are the products of the author's imagination. The opinions expressed in this book do not seek to reflect the views of the Publisher.*

Dedicated to

My Dear Parents

who always thought that my Initiatives

are Worthy!

Special thanks to Indian Railways for

Memorable Journeys!

Contents

One More Beggar

Old Delhi is always foggy in the month of January. Winter kills numerous lives every year in Delhi. One cold morning around 9 am I step down at old Delhi station. I quickly came out of the station building and started walking towards metro station. My eyes were reading that giant letters of DELHI written in Urdu which were hanging on the old red coloured station building.

Off course, it was not my first time, but, Old Delhi Station has its own charm! Suddenly, one old shivering voice interrupted my amusement, "Bhaiya, can you please dial one number? I am lost! I want to talk to my Son!". My eyes were rolling up and down on that Lady. She must be nearly 65 years old, wearing dirty saree and only one shawl in the freezing cold! She had one simple old bag with her.

I was getting late. But I couldn't refuse to help her. I dialled number on my smartphone and handed it over to her. As, I was standing next to her, I was able to listen to their conversation clearly. She literally got excited when his son received the call, "hello beta, I am at old Delhi station. where are you? Will you come to pick me up? Did your brother call you? He dropped me here and returned back in next train. I am lost . . ."

Before she completes, man shouted from other side, "Are you mad or what? Who told you to come here? I don't have any capacity to feed you. Ask your son to take you back with him. He didn't inform me anything about you...." He kept on insulting her mother. His furious voice was really arrogant. After hardly one-minute conversation phone call got disconnected (actually her son disconnected). I gave a blank look at her face as if I didn't listen anything.

Instead of returning my phone, she asked me to dial one more number. Her eyes were almost in tears. Her voice had urge and helplessness. I started dialling another number without uttering a single word. She waited for 10 seconds and another male voice responded to the call, "Hello, who is this?". She said "beta, I am stuck at the station and your brother..." And there was a sound of “Beep… beep… beep.” on the phone. Her another son bluntly cut the call. After freezing for five seconds She wiped up her tears and requested me to call on the same number again. I did so and nobody answered the call. "One more time please!" And I called again.

Repeatedly, for 5 times I called on that number and her son intentionally didn't respond. She dropped down her head sadly and returned my phone. She moved her legs slowly without knowing where to go! Her tears finally rolled out on her old loose face skin. I was shocked and she was broken.

I looked at my phone screen and realised the time. Then, I ran towards the metro station. While running I turned back to check where that lady was going. Apparently, she was out from sight in dull white fog. Thousands of questions and thoughts about that lady were disturbing my mind. I don't know why but I was feeling guilty. May be because one more Beggar was added to the Old Delhi Station or may be one more name was about to be added on to Delhi Winter's Death List.

Remember: You can't reverse the Time.

Live Now!

The Thief

Do you know what is so relaxing? When you have just one bag to keep eyes upon, confirmed sleeper coach seat and a whole night journey!

I had boarded Somnath - Jabalpur Express from Anand Junction at around 8 30 pm to reach Bhopal Station next morning. My seat number was in second compartment from the door of sleeper coach. Passengers in my compartment were enjoying dinner. They were exchanging food items and even offered me. As I already had heavy dinner, there was no need to chew anything else. I thanked them for the offer and refused kindly. Without any chit-chat I climbed upon my Upper berth, removed shoes and placed it on the twin fans, pulled out my phone from pocket and enjoyed songs for half an hour (oh, I had earphone).

Gradually, lights in all compartments were turning off. Within couple of hours sleeper coach was totally dark. I also removed earphone and closed my eyes. After a long time, I was enjoying peaceful sleep as a railway passenger. Just like any horror movie, at midnight I heard a loud scream of female voice. I fearfully opened up my eyes and got up on my berth. Similarly, other passengers also woke up and turned on lights to solve the mystery.

It took no time to identify the lady who had screamed. She was around thirty-five-year-old wearing kurta and jeans. She was completely in shock as if she had encountered an evil spirit! She was sitting on lower side seat of first compartment just next to the door of sleeper coach. Crowd of passengers surrounded her and asked the matter. I jumped down from my upper seat and joined the crowd to know the story. We all had lines of anxiety on our faces.

She claimed that one unknown guy came near to her seat from washroom area and pulled out one small bag which she was using as a pillow and resting her head upon. Due to sudden attack, she screamed loudly and before she could grab that person in the dark, he jumped down from door on railway track with that small bag. We were clear that, thief must have broken his hands or legs while jumping from speedily running train.

Usually, when a passenger uses bag as a pillow, bag may carry valuable costly items or any important documents. Now, we were curious to know what she has lost! One old gentleman asked her, "what was there in your Bag?". Lady replied, "One Packet of Mamara."

(Mamara is a Guajarati snack food made from rice).

After a pause of one second, everyone started giggling except that lady. Mood of crowd suddenly got changed. Now, the sympathy of passengers was shifted to thief from lady! Everyone started assuming how many fractures that thief might be having for a cost of One Packet of Mamara!!!

Happiness = Confirm Train Ticket!

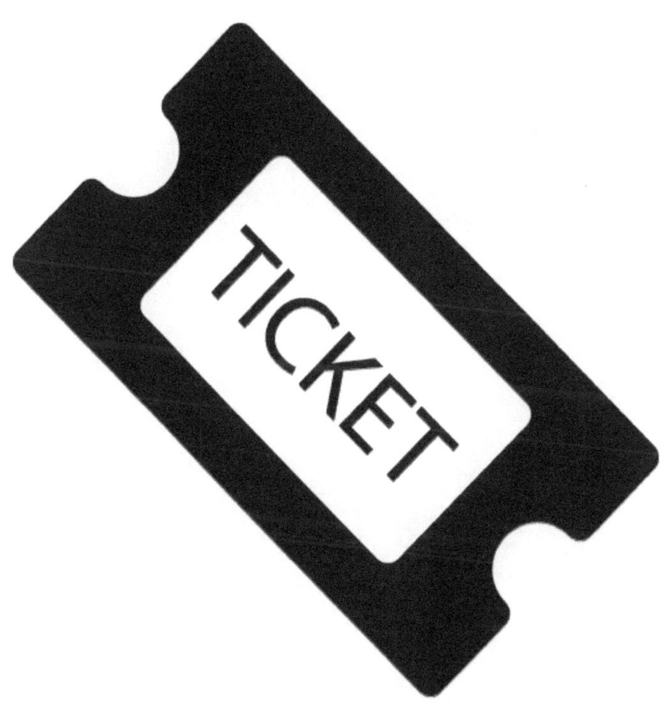

Law Abiding Citizen

The funniest and most boring character in any train journey is always performed by that one rigid mid age uncle (Actually hiding his old age with hair colour).

I was traveling back to Gujarat from Mumbai through Shatabdi Express. Surprisingly, due to heavy rain half of the seats were unoccupied in my coach. Still, my fate was strong enough to bless me with one uncle sitting in same chair compartment at aisle side seat. I was enjoying the thunderstorm and beauty of nature outside the window. Thinking about how lucky I was to get a window seat journey in such a rainy weather!

Dark clouds and lighting of thunder were leading my imagination to the grand Entry of Prince Thor! At the same time, heavy rain above the Train was disturbing that old age uncle! I suddenly looked over my left shoulder and my eyes observed that irritated uncle keenly.

There was a leak in the roof of train and drops were falling exactly on uncle's seat. His mood was spoiled. He was not able to use his cell phone, eat his food, carry his small bag in lap or even to put a fake smile on his face! I smiled at him sarcastically. He ignored my smile while saving his healthy old body from next drop of water attacking from upside.

I couldn't understand why he was not changing his seat! There were almost 20 more vacant seats around him! What can be the reason of sticking here? Maybe he was enjoying to peep in my phone when I was watching video songs. Maybe he didn't take bath in the morning and now loved to get wet with cold drops! Before I assumed third weird reason, ticket checker asked my name. I gently informed, "Shardul Dave". he gave me a blunt look and ticked on paper carelessly. He didn't ask anything to that annoyed old age uncle. May be his face was only reflecting anger and TC didn't find it proper to ask him a single question.

TC took his first step towards the next compartment and old age uncle gripped his wrist tightly. TC and I, we both were scared! Presuming that, uncle would complaint about leaking roof and would start endless arguments. contradictorily, well-educated uncle politely said," Sir, can I please change the seat! I am done with this water drops! You can check my seat it's all . . . " TC interrupted, "sir, half of the train is empty, you can sit wherever you want!". That old man replied, "but, I was waiting for you. Without your permission, being a responsible citizen, I shouldn't change my seat. Thank you. Thank you, sir, for allowing me!" Now this time, lines of worries on his face turned into a happy smile! He quickly got up and changed his seat! I laughed to myself at his silly act soundlessly.

I focused again on my video songs and 3D animation type natural scenery outside! After thirty seconds, one more thought passed by my mind, "he wasn't fool, he wasn't rigid, he was a law-abiding Citizen!".

Map Route may Misguide you;

Railway Tracks Never!

Spark in Your Eyes!

"Oh God, railway ticket queues are really hectic and those who breaks the ticket queue are just worst! I lost my rifle shooting match today and now I would not be able to catch my train even! Complete waste of time, ticket money, energy and a day!" Such disruptive thoughts were running on my mind. At the same speed, Train which I wanted to catch was departing in front of my eyes from platform number 03 of Ahmedabad station. I was standing on platform number 01 and there was a railway track in between.

My anger suddenly burst out in form of energy. I decided to catch the train at any cost. I made a strong grip on my rifle box and started running towards the ladder. It was a shocking action for passengers standing around to see a young boy running like a Milkha with rifle in his hands. I literally didn't care about hurting people that evening. I kept running until I reached platform number 03.

My train was still far to my legs but it was clearly visible to my sight. It was slowly catching speed. My furious mind again refused to let it go! I ran for the train madly. Unfortunately, before I could reach to the door of last passenger coach, train speed defeated my panting lungs.

Unexpectedly, signaller of train offered me a helping hand to catch the train! (For a moment, situation reminded me 'JA SIMRAN JA . . .' Scene) Somehow, I managed to be on the last coach of the train - the coach of the guard. We both went inside the coach. It was like a small room. Few signal flags, one old radio, pages of newspaper, half-filled water bottle and the signaller. I put down my rifle box and relaxed my body. He offered me water and asked me few questions. Who are you? Where are you going? Why did you come late? Ultimately, after a usual conversation, we both decided that at next station I will shift to passenger coach.

Still there was some time left to reach next station, we continued our conversation. I asked him curiously, "the way you helped me, you must be helping many people to catch their train everyday right?". He denied by nodding his head. Further, I asked, "Then, why did you help me?". He replied, "See, it's not my duty to help anybody to catch the train. Every day, I see number of faces running behind train. They all are tired, sad and demoralised people. Their faces reflect worries and tension. I am seriously tired of watching them every day. When I saw you, I didn't think you will keep running behind the train. But you did. when you were just about to catch the train, it increased its speed. Normally, people make weird faces and stop running. But, instead of showcasing a hopelessness, your face was shining with anger and determination. Your eyes had some spark. So, I thought of helping you!"

I got down at next station to change my coach with a smile of satisfaction. I thanked signaller for everything. That day, May be my eyes lost the shooting match, but, for sure it won the signaller's heart.

(Solo) Travelling teaches you everything!

Rich Dads

Indian Local trains are famous for two things. One is heavy crowd and second is delayed arrival! One tedious summer afternoon, I was suffering from both. Local train was halted on side railway track to make an uninterrupted way for superfast express train. The way potato boil in cooker, I was boiling in local train coach with other passengers. Undoubtedly, with non-negotiable fragrance of numerous sweaty bodies.

As majority of the youngsters do, I was listening to random music with earphones to avoid the scenario around me. Meanwhile, I got red signal from mobile phone battery. To save my mobile battery, I kept my phone in pocket and moved my eyes here and there in search of live entertainment.

Unwillingly, group of labourers caught my attention. They were bunch of five people sitting on my opposite three sitter seat (it's officially three sitters, otherwise, people know the reality). Their dirty faces, clothes and luggage were confirming that they were construction site workers. They were constantly talking in their own language slang and disturbing others.

After ten fifteen minutes of passive listening, I started understanding their conversation. Simultaneously, train also moved slowly and again stopped on next station within five minutes. Passengers literally jumped down on platform to get water bottles and food. Within no time, small station turned into any zombie film set up! Cold drink sellers and other train vendors also entered inside the train. They were happy as crowd was hungry and thirsty enough! One Batatawada (snacks) seller passed by my compartment. Those workers shouted and called him back. They individually paid for their batatawada dishes. Each plate costs Ten rupees. Notably, only one worker didn't buy food or water. Others were forcing him to eat. but he denied.

I was staring at him while eating my last batatawada from paper plate. Labour next to him asked him unpleasantly in their language, "why don't you eat anything? Since morning we had nothing and further, we don't know when we will reach. Don't you feel hungry?" After a second that hungry labour opened up his mouth and left me in amusing surprise. He said, "I am not single like you all! My kid was crying a lot to get a chocolate when I met him last time. So, today I will surely give him a ten rupees' big chocolate. Also, I am not that much hungry today!".

My hands gripped on to empty plate of Batatawada tightly. Without blinking my eyes, I continued starring at a rich humble father with respect.

May be Indian local trains are special because countless rich dads are travelling through it daily with immense love in heart for their kids.

Want to test your patience?

Try Railway Ticket Queue!

Chappal Story

Indian Railways not only facilitate daily movement to mass of Employees but, also cater to range of Job seekers traveling for career opportunities! Few jobseekers get back to their homes with happy faces and few with broken hearts. That evening, I was among the second category of job seekers. Hustled for almost fourteen hours and finally got rejected in second last round of selection process.

With thousands of demoralised thoughts, I boarded half empty Ahmedabad Vadodara local Train. My legs were tired, eyes were sleepy and mind was frustrated. My shirt has started adopting smell of my sweaty body. With such negative condition, my train journey began.

I wanted to put full stop on happenings around, I had enough of uncertainties on the day! Out of nowhere, I heard loud noise of crowd standing near the door. After a minute I understood scenario, one mid age lady tried to catch the moving train and was about to fall down. But, somehow people near door dragged her inside. Her left leg chappal was missing and her blood pressure was high like anything. She was breathing like old railway's steam engine. People Settled her on my opposite seat. I firmly believe that one should only help others if their own stomach is full. As, I was hungry as hell, I didn't Console her. But kind crowd continued taking care of her.

That lady was disappointed and angry on own self. Hazardous incident also disturbed her totally. After few minutes she also noticed that she was wearing only right leg chappal. She was searching furiously for missing chappal. After failing for search, with double anger she removed her right leg chappal and threw it out of the window. People around observed her act but, didn't asked her anything.

One college boy entered to the coach from connecting way of another coach. He had one chappal in his hand and his eyes were constantly searching for someone. He saw that mid age lady and gave her that chappal. He informed that he saw entire incident and how she boarded the train. He was behind that lady only. Thus, he lifted up chappal from platform which fell down while going through struggle of entering inside and entered to the next coach. Then, he came there to find that lady to return her chappal. Lady's frustration level gone ten to hundred. Because, just few minutes back she threw away one chappal and now she is having second one in her hand. After that boy disappeared in crowd, that lady even threw away even another chappal (same as she did first time). Anyway, her chappal pair won't be completed.

Her stupid and impatient behaviour cost her loss of I pair of chappal. She should have kept another chappal and waited for some time. Then, definitely her pair of chappal would have completed.

I was already drained out of my energy. Still, I got the philosophical interpretation from this whole incident. I must keep chappal of determination and hard work with me. Another chappal of opportunity and success will definitely come back. I smiled and enjoyed the rest of the train journey with my favourite songs!

Sweaty Struggle is Temporary;

Keep Smiling!!!

On the Bench

Many times, you don't miss the train, train miss arrival timing! In such cases, platforms may look overcrowded. Passengers get unnecessarily excited whenever any train (even Goods train) cross that station. "Is it my Train?" This major question always keeps confusing passengers. Honestly, nobody trusts the announcement makers who keep informing in three languages that train is late but, it will arrive in few minutes." May be such announcements has disappointed many passengers in past!

On one burning afternoon, my train missed the arrival timings. I was on railway platform and was waiting for impatient people to get up from their bench and bent down on the railway track to check that from which side train engine was whistling! Off course I had strong intentions to grab their sitting space. With the grace of God, I succeeded in my plan.

I finally got a place to sit on middle seat of aluminium three sitter bench. I felt relaxed. Right side seat was occupied by typical Indian Uncle. My left side seat was occupied by one mid age modern lady. That lady wasn't alone. After few minutes I realized that her husband was standing near to railway track impatiently and I was the one who snatched away his seat. That couple was very young. Their ages must be below thirty. Well, everything is fair when you are an Indian middle-class tired traveller and that too in the season of sun.

May be God had other plans. Within no time Indian uncle started leaning down his head on my right shoulder! He was sleepy like anything! I was not at all ready to handle that!

I gently asked him to sit straight. But, another two minutes, and same thing happened! On the other side that lady called her husband and loudly started scolding him for leaving his place. So that I can listen to it and leave that bench. (As uncle Ben said to Spider man) 'With great powers comes great responsibility'. I got a seat but with mental torture by lady and weight of old age uncle's head.

In between, my frustration level had Crossed the bearing capacity. I made an instant action plan to mitigate that situation. Third time, uncle carelessly rested his head on my right shoulder. I didn't hesitate. I acted like a statue for two more minutes and uncle transferred all upper body weight on my right-side body. Meanwhile, on left side, lady was constantly barking in my ears.

I took a deep breath and with a speed of light, i stood up from that bench. As gravity and sleep both exited, uncle fell down on lady's lap. He fearfully opened his eyes and fearfully said, "Sorry... sorry... sorry Aunty! I am really sorry!" people around observed that and started laughing. As, uncle's age was nearly double to lady's age!

I started jumping on platform with 'LOL'ness on my face. That Aunty, ohh, I mean lady finally gave a break to her tongue out of embarrassment. Before her husband could release his legs, I again took the same place. I closed my eyes and smiled as if nothing had happened!

Railway Platforms are more exciting than Trains!

Sweaty Dreams

Sometimes you don't hope for seat! You just wish to make enough space to enter and stand inside the general coach of express train. I wished same while looking at overcrowded express train. Each person standing inside was sweaty. It was difficult to breathe in there. But, my love for wrestling enabled me to get into crowded coach! For sure, there were greater number of people standing inside compared to people on seat! I was mentally ready to face the inconvenience for next couple of hours.

After few minutes, newly boarded passengers adjusted with old passengers. Train caught speed and fresh air from windows helped me to breath. Gradually, noise of voices slowed down. I realized that I was surrounded by three friends. I was standing at centre point and blocking their conversation. But they seemed to know each other for a long time. They ignored my physical existence and continued their talk. About Job, about boss, about family, about house loan, about new shirt, about morning train journey, about another common friend and about. . .Their talks were really endless! Undauntedly, I was listening each word! I had no choice! I was not able to move my hands even. It's totally risky to pull out hands-free. No one knows at which moment it may get broken in such overcrowded place!

(Let's name those three friends Ramesh, Suresh and Mahesh)

After a while, Ramesh asked to Suresh, "hey, you wanted to go on a trip with your wife, right? What happened?" To which Suresh

Replied, "Yes I do want to but.... we have to set up our home first! So, we are investing into the house hold items. May be next year we can go on a trip!" Mahesh interrupted, "I too wanted to go on a trip, but, house rent, parents' medical treatment expenses and other regular household spending makes it impossible to gather enough money to travel. Moreover, my house is in need of renovation! So, I need to bare that unexpected cost also this year!" One after another, each friend started listing their expenses!

As any moderator conclude discussion, Suresh gave the closing speech for that traveling topic, "We are traveling in the same train since last five years and keep talking about going on holidays every season. But our responsibilities aren't allowing us to move away from our routine. Our limited salary is not fitting to unlimited expenses. Still somehow, we are managing enough for our survival! You know friends, we are going to follow the same routine till we die, same train, same job and more responsibilities."

That speech hit me hard, my soul said to my mind, "Life is too short! Go on a trip my boy! Maybe, later means never!" Though, I knew each future responsibility, their conversation scared me! Very next moment, I decided to travel as much as possible! That's how, I decided to fulfil my sweaty dreams!

Be the Engine of your Dream Life!

Jugadu Passenger

No matter which train it is! No matter which season it is! You can always find at least one family traveling to attend marriage function! Without that, no train coach is complete. Sometimes, you may also find silent solo passengers wearing expensive outfits traveling to attend the marriage!

One fine day my bestie got married (finally!!!) After a 'Well Planned' goodbye, I headed back towards my hometown. Fortunately, I got the seat in local train. There are few creatures who loves to hang on doors of train coach even though there was a space inside!

Bunch of regular travellers standing near door were constantly staring at me with shocking lines on face! Once I put off my navy-blue blazer and set down on seat, leader of that group asked me, "Are you a ticket checker?" I said, "No". one another group member lying upon luggage rack above my head added, "oh, your dark blue suit and your personality gave us Vibes that you are a ticket checker. Thank God, you are not!" Before I could assume that they were traveling with or without ticket, group leader confessed that they didn't had tickets. He also explained his past experiences of being caught by ticket checker and still he continues to travel every day without ticket.

His brown hair and healthy face didn't allow my mind to consider him as a poor guy! But, according to him, he was just a worker earning little daily wages and didn't have money to buy a ticket every day. Instead of that he prefers to spend money only after (if) getting caught by ticket checker. It was comparatively costing lower amount than purchasing tickets every day. After that, he again started pulling legs of other group members and continued enjoying the journey with senseless naughty jokes! He was definitely humble, extrovert and influential personality (At least among group members)! But I was really not impressed. His such mentality about traveling without ticket was really unfair and against law as per me and as per railway rules as well. I had already developed disrespect for that man.

Nearly forty-five minutes later, I took up my bag and stepped down on my hometown railway platform! I felt relaxed after an exhausted day! Your hometown platform always gives you a homely feeling, right! Out of nowhere, somebody gently covered my shoulders with blazer. I turned around and surprisingly he was that man! That unethical group leader! He said, "you forget that blazer in train, Mr. ticket checker". I smiled and thanked him for returning my blazer!

Train wheels had already started moving. I asked him, "So, I got my blazer back, but you missed your friends, remaining journey you need to complete alone!" He laughed and answered, "I don't earn much money. but I have many friends!" The way Usain Bolt runs towards finish line, he disappeared into random coach of running train!

His words inspired me a lot! I don’t know who he was! but, He has made unique space in my heart. I couldn't Stop smiling for next few minutes! He was an unethical, cheerful and talkative man or may be just a Jugadu Passenger!

Interestingly,

T·C· always travel without Ticket!

"May be Never . . ."

Traveling in sleeping coaches are like classroom journey. Initially, you meet few strangers, feel insecure and uncomfortable. Gradually you get a homely feeling with them. You talk, exchange food, know each other's destinations, native places, names, professions and purposes. Simultaneously, you build a trust. At the end you say goodbye to each other with a smile and hope for meeting again!

Same way I was traveling in Jammu - Tavi Express to reach pathankot. I was comfortably traveling with fellow travellers on my lower side seat of sleeper coach. I had already spent thirteen plus hours on same seat from last evening.

Around 10 am, fortunately, there were no naughty kids and suspicious individuals nearby to my seat. So, I step down on one Platform to fill my bottle with fresh cold water. I returned to my train coach before departure timing and saw one tall man blocking my seat. He took my mobile from my seat and started speaking, "is this your phone? Why did you put it here on seat? It is not safe! You should take care of your things. I was waiting for you to return so that i can step down to purchase water." I was responding his questions non verbally by nodding my head. It felt like my elder brother is yelling at me for some misconduct. I was happy though, for safety of my phone.

My eyes didn't fail to recognise his identity. His green full sleeve t shirt, his haircut, well maintained body, Hindi words with tone of military and his cap! He was an Indian army

Soldier who Settled himself silently on upper seat of my seat without disturbing my sleep last night.

Train wheels started rolling again and I insisted him to sit with me on my lower seat. I asked and confirm about his Identity. He has boarded train from Jaipur to reach and report his senior at J&K (old) Indo-Pak border. I asked him about routine on border area. He was really surviving through a tough condition. He described me casually about his long duty hours, counter firing incidents, his fauji buddy, newly joined officer of his unit and also about four to five hours sleep per day. I already wanted to talk more about life at borders. But, to divert the conversation I curiously asked about his experience during his leave time at his home in Rajasthan.

He informed me that, during twenty days leaves he used to train youngsters every morning 4 am to 8 am for joining army. He trained them for running and other exercises.

He was a well-accepted role model for defence aspirants from his village. I was impressed with his selfless attitude and hardworking spirit. Also felt bad that now his leave had been cancelled by his superiors and he didn't get enough time to spent with his better half (oh, he recently got married during his leave period). Also, he explained that it's very difficult to get a train ticket at last moment and unlike other countries, Indian soldiers are not allowed to wear uniform during return traveling to avoid misuse of it.

I was feeling like reading an adventurous novel while talking to him. But, one uncle adjusted himself on opposite seat and disrupted our talk. To join our talk, he loudly said, "I just don't like such train journeys, it's already two hours late! I don't know at what time I will reach home tonight! What do you think so when will you reach back to home?"

Soldier smiled sarcastically on uncle's silly complaint. He said, "I don't know! Maybe, I will never get back to my home!" Uncle didn't understand his answer. But I did.

Thanks to Indian Railways for such fabulous journeys and thanks to our all the soldiers for their spirit for motherland and keeping "Service Before Self".

Message to Readers

Hi, this is Shardul. Thank you so much for reading my experiences! I hope you liked my real-life Incidents!

Now, I am eagerly waiting to read your reviews/ comments/ opinions . . .

My Email Id is **sharduldave13@gmail.com**

You may also share your memories of Railway traveling.

If you are a Happy Reader of Local Passenger then don't forget to attach your selfie with the book!

ABOUT THE AUTHOR

MBA, Traveling and Indianness completely summarise Shardul Dave. He was honoured twice with Governor's Medal for his extraordinary performance as an NCC Cadet at National and International Level.

He is from Anand, Gujarat.

Apart from following corporate life routine, Shardul is actively engaged in various adventure, camping and creative writing activities for more than a decade.

You can Follow on...

sharduldave13@gmail.com

shardul.dave

www.facebook.com/sharduldave013

www.ingramcontent.com/pod-product-compliance
Lightning Source LLC
LaVergne TN
LVHW050421160726
843469LV00041B/1183

* 9 7 8 9 3 5 4 1 6 8 3 1 4 *